feldman fieldmouse
a fable

by
Nathaniel Benchley

drawings by **Hilary Knight**

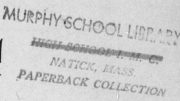

A HARPER TROPHY BOOK
Harper & Row, Publishers

NEW YORK

EVANSTON

SAN FRANCISCO

LONDON

FOR CLAYTON
A friend to all fieldmice

FELDMAN FIELDMOUSE. Text copyright © 1971 by Nathaniel
Benchley. Illustrations copyright © 1971 by Hilary Knight. All
rights reserved. No part of this book may be used or reproduced
in any manner whatsoever without written permission except in
the case of brief quotations embodied in critical articles and re-
views. Printed in the United States of America. For information
address Harper & Row, Publishers, Inc., 10 East 53rd Street, New
York, N.Y. 10022. Published simultaneously in Canada by
Fitzhenry & Whiteside Limited, Toronto.

Standard Book Number 06-440032-8
First printed in 1971. 3rd printing, 1972.

I

"We have mice," Lonny Stebbins' mother announced, coming into the kitchen. "I thought we'd got rid of them."

"How do you know?" his father asked. "Have you seen any?"

"There are plenty of ways to tell," Mrs. Stebbins replied darkly. "Among other things, there are tooth marks on the onions."

"I made those marks," Lonny said from his seat at the kitchen table. "I like to nibble at onions."

"I'll tell you one thing, young man," his mother said. "Any more wild stories out of you, and you won't get that bicycle."

The Stebbins family — Lonny, his father, and his mother — lived outside a town far from

5

the city. There was a pond and a brook and woods, and in the summer Lonny sometimes rode a neighbor's horse around a field beyond the pond; but the one thing he wanted more than anything was a bicycle, so he could ride into town. It was a dull walk, and even hitch-hiking took a long time, and he felt that if he had a bicycle he would have all the mobility of an eagle. The only problem was that his birth-day came in November; it was now early spring, and the matter of the bicycle would be held over his head for the next six months at least. To be-have perfectly for six months was, he felt, more than should be asked of anyone, but it seemed the only way. After that, Christmas would be such a letdown as to be barely worth observing.

"That is not a wild story," Lonny said quietly. "I like to nibble onions."

"With the skins on?" his mother asked.

"Yes," he replied, looking directly at her.

"Well, we'll see about the mice," his father said. "If traps don't work, then I'll put some mouse seed around."

"Just do the mouse seed," said Mrs. Steb-bins. "I hate traps."

"So do the mice," said Lonny.

His parents looked at him queerly, and for a few moments there was silence. Then his father turned to his mother. "Where should I put the seed?" he asked. "I don't think it's very smart to strew poison in our own food bin."

"I saw traces in the back room," Mrs. Stebbins replied. "Just put it around where you think they might be."

Mr. Stebbins considered this. "That's a pretty loose order," he said at last. "I'll have to give it some thought."

"Think all you want," said Mrs. Stebbins as she began to prepare lunch. "Just get rid of the mice, is all I ask."

After lunch Lonny wandered into the back room, which was a kind of catch-all place for storing odds and ends. There were packing cases and canned goods and hip boots; there was a gold-framed picture of Mrs. Stebbins' Aunt Felicity, which was dusted off and hung in the parlor every Thanksgiving, when the wispy, birdlike lady came for dinner; there was fishing tackle and wrapping paper and the bin that held both onions and potatoes; and in one corner was a large, old, rolltop desk, in which were letters and papers and bills and insurance policies and things that Mr. Stebbins didn't really want but didn't want to throw away. The top of the desk was kept closed, pulled down like a rattling, wooden window shade, to keep the things inside from falling on the floor. Lonny looked in the onion bin, picked up an onion and examined the tiny tooth marks that had sliced their way through the outer skin, then turned it over and took a bite himself. The skin was like crisp paper, but the onion tasted strong and sweet. He was about to take another bite when he heard a faint rustling noise, like someone crumbling dried leaves, and it had a quick and frantic rhythm. He looked around to see what was making the noise, but he could see nothing, and then he realized it was coming from the desk. He approached slowly, not sure what to expect, and by careful listening he narrowed down the spot to one desk drawer. He opened it a crack, then pulled it out all the way, and there on the far inside was a mouse, surrounded by shredded paper and busily eating the last of an old and yellowed insurance policy.

"Hey!" Lonny exclaimed. "Look here!"

The mouse stopped eating and glanced up at him with small, black eyes, then resumed its chewing, as though to get the last few bites before trouble started. Actually, Lonny realized, it was shredding the paper to make a nest, because it would have taken a dozen mice to eat the mounds of nibbled paper that filled the drawer.

"Look where?" his father asked, coming into the room. "What've you found?" Lonny showed him the drawer, and Mr. Stebbins' eyes grew wide. "Well, I'll be a flat-bottomed canal barge!" he shouted. "He's gone and eaten up my papers!" The mouse, sensing that the time had come to depart, flicked up over the edge of the drawer and vanished. Mr. Stebbins tossed the shredded paper in the air, then pulled open another drawer. It, too, was full of tiny scraps, and two mice zipped out of sight into the back of the desk. Every drawer he opened had held at least one nesting mouse, and when he rolled back the top of the desk it looked as though he had let loose a pile of snow. Startled mice peeked out from mounds of paper and then disappeared, and suddenly the desk seemed to itch with the sounds

of scrabbling mouse feet. "Mice!" Mr. Stebbins roared, above the noise of the fleeing animals. "They've eaten us out of house and home!"

Mrs. Stebbins came into the room, wiping her hands on a dish towel. "I told you they were here," she said. "But you wouldn't believe me."

"You may be congratulated," her husband said more calmly. "You were one hundred percent right. You were one thousand and thirty-seven percent right. In fact, what I admire most was your understatement."

"There's no need for sarcasm," she replied. "Just get rid of them, is all I ask."

Lonny helped his father clean out the desk. Then Mr. Stebbins went into town and returned with several boxes of what looked like birdseed but was actually poison. He tore a small hole in each box, so that the seed would run out, and then he put them inside the desk and in the drawers and two or three places around the room. Lonny watched him in silence.

"Do you have to kill them?" he asked at last. "Isn't it enough to just frighten them away?"

"Frighten them away and they'll only come back," his father replied. "Mice don't remember anything for long."

Next day the mouse seed was strewn about, which meant that the mice had been into it, and the next day even more so. Then, after the floor had been swept, it remained clean and no more seed was scattered about, which meant the seed had done its work.

A week or so later, Lonny got off the school bus and walked slowly up the path to his house. It was the first day that had really felt like spring; the earth was moist and sweet-smelling, there were yellow bursts of Forsythia near the woods, and the trees were lacy and bright green. From nearby came the ringing of the brook, where the cold water tumbled over white stones on its way into the pond. Lonny reached the front steps and sat down, letting the sun bathe his face. It felt so good he unzipped his jacket, and he was about to take it off when he saw, in the new grass beside the steps, something so small that he had to look twice to make sure what it was. It was a mouse, no bigger than the end of his thumb, and it was so young that it seemed to be all head, with transparent pink hind feet and tight-shut eyes. Lonny expected it to move, but it didn't; it just crouched, quivering, in the grass, and waited. How it got there he couldn't tell, but it was clearly lost and waiting for its mother, who was nowhere to be seen. Very carefully, Lonny reached down and cupped his hands under it and lifted it to his face, and looking at it closely he could see the shiny pink ears, the mouth the size of a pinprick, and the forepaws like little snips of thread. He took it inside, where his mother was in the kitchen.

"Look what I found," he said.

His mother looked into his cupped and dirty hands, stared, and said, "Oh my. Where?"

"In the grass, by the front steps."

Still looking at the mouse, Mrs. Stebbins said, "It's cold, poor baby. And probably hungry. You didn't see its mother?"

"No. It was all alone. May I keep it?"

There was a long pause while his mother looked at the mouse, and then she said, "If you think you can save it. You might do better to put it back, and hope its mother'll find it."

"Its mother wasn't there!" Lonny insisted.

"Besides, it'll be dark pretty soon and nobody will find it, and it'll starve and freeze to death! We have to keep it here!"

His mother took a deep breath. "All right," she said. "But you'll be the one who has to feed it."

"That's easy! We've got cheese, and — onions, and —"

"It's much too young for that. You've got to feed it milk. Warm milk, and probably with an eyedropper."

"All right. You warm some milk, and I'll get a box and cotton and an eyedropper, and fix it up a nest." Lonny set the mouse on the kitchen table and ran from the room, and his mother looked for almost a minute at the small gray thing on the table. Then she sighed, took some milk from the refrigerator, and began to warm it on the stove.

When Mr. Stebbins got home, Lonny was crouched over a cotton-lined box and was pointing an eyedropper at something inside, saying, "There! He just took another!" Mr. Stebbins went and peered over his son's shoulder.

"What's going on?" he asked.

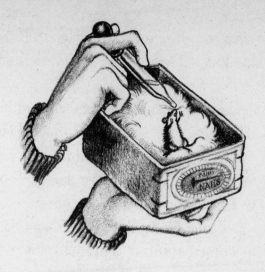

"It's a baby mouse," Lonny replied, not looking up. "I found him outside and Mother said I could keep him if I fed him, so I've made a nest and now he's taking milk from the dropper. Don't come too close, or you'll frighten him."

Mr. Stebbins turned to his wife, who was busy at the stove. "Are you crazy?" he asked.

"No," she replied, looking into the steaming pot in front of her. "I said he could keep it if he took care of it."

"But these are the things we kill when they're bigger — in fact, you're the one who asks me to kill them!"

"That makes no difference," Mrs. Stebbins replied, speaking to the stove. "This one is little."

Mr. Stebbins rolled his eyes heavenward and went to the sink, where he began to wash his hands. "All right," he said, twirling the soap between his palms. "But next time don't ask me to be the executioner. I don't get any more pleasure out of that kind of thing than you do."

"There won't be a next time," Lonny said. "I'm in charge of what's going on here, and I can talk to mice."

"Remember about the wild stories," his mother put in, with a warning tone.

"There's nothing wild about talking to mice," Lonny said, as he squeezed out another drop of milk. "The real trick is to get them to talk to you." The mouse's lips gathered in the milk, and Lonny said, "Isn't that right, Charlie? I think I'll call him Charlie."

"It's even odds you ought to call it Charlotte," his father said, reaching for a towel. "And after that, I hate to think."

II

The mouse grew fast, and pretty soon was eating anything that Lonny gave it. He fed it cheese and crackers and peanut butter and onions and sunflower seeds and apples and dry oatmeal and cookies, and the mouse took a little bit of everything he gave it, sniffing first and then nibbling quickly if the smell seemed right. He fed it so much that it got fat and lazy, and would sometimes eat only if Lonny put the food directly in its mouth. The mouse slept a lot, its whiskers twitching as it dreamed.

Then one morning Lonny came downstairs and found his parents grim-faced in the kitchen. He knew something was wrong, and he looked quickly at the nest, and saw the mouse asleep. "What's happened?" he asked.

"The time has come," his father said. "The mouse has got to go."

Something closed in Lonny's throat. "Why?" he said. "What did he do?"

"He got out. He's been all over the kitchen and into the onion bin and nobody knows where else. Pretty soon he'll attract more mice, and we'll be right back where we started. The time to get rid of him is now."

Lonny was barely able to speak. "Are you going to kill him?" he asked.

"No, of course not," his mother said gently. "We just think you'd better put him outside, where you found him, and let him fend for himself. After all, he is a fieldmouse, and he ought to be in the fields."

"But he CAN'T fend for himself!" Lonny cried. "He doesn't know how!"

"He'll learn," his father said. "No mouse ever starved to death."

"He doesn't know where to look! I've fed him everything he's ever eaten, and without me he won't know what to do! Or the Bigelows' cat will get him, or — ".

"That's the way it goes," his father said. "Animals can't expect people to look after them all."

"But he isn't all animals — he's mine! Suppose I build a cage for him — can I keep him then?"

After a long pause, his mother said, "Well —" and his father sighed, and Lonny knew he'd won.

"Here we go," his father said. "I was going to spade up the garden, but now it looks as though I'll be building a mouse cage."

"I'll do it," Lonny said.

"You'd better let me," replied his father. "We want to make sure he doesn't get out."

In the back room they found a glass tank that had once held goldfish, and they put the mouse nest in this and covered it over with wire from an old screen door. Then Mr. Stebbins put a brass ashtray on top of the wire as a weight, and stood back to survey his work.

"That ought to keep him in," he said with satisfaction. "Any mouse that gets out of that will have to be a magician."

When his father had gone into the garden, Lonny went to the cupboard and got a ginger cookie, then took the top off the tank and crumbled the cookie in front of the mouse. The mouse sniffed once and began to eat, and after a moment Lonny heard a strange squeak. The mouse stopped eating and squeaked again, and Lonny bent down until his head was almost in the tank and said, "What did you say?"

"I said 'thank you,'" squeaked the mouse.

For almost a minute Lonny didn't move; he stayed crouched over the tank with one ear cocked toward the mouse while he watched it devour the cookie. He couldn't believe what he'd heard, but it had seemed very clear, and he was almost afraid to try again for fear he might have made a mistake. Finally he could stand it no longer. "Can you talk?" he asked in a low voice.

"To you," the mouse replied, brushing off its whiskers.

"And did you just say 'thank you?'"

"Yes. I'd never have been able to live outside. This is much nicer here. That makes twice you've saved my life."

"Do you mind if we keep you penned up like this?"

"Not at all. So long as you feed me, I don't need to go anywhere."

"Where did you go last night?"

"That wasn't me. That was Uncle Feldman."

"Who?"

"Uncle Feldman. He comes to see me nights, and tells me what's going on outside. From what he says, I'm much better off where I am."

"Where does he live?"

The mouse paused. "He doesn't want it known," it said at last. "He's the only member of the family left, and he's being pretty careful now."

"Was that your family who lived in the desk?"

"So he says. I was just born, so I don't remember much about it."

"What's your name?"

"Uncle Feldman says my parents called me Fendall. Fendall Fieldmouse. But they're all dead, so you can call me what you like."

"I was calling you Charlie, but I think I like Fendall better. Is that all right?"

"It's fine with me," said Fendall. "One name is as good as the next, as far as I'm concerned."

"I'm sorry about your parents," Lonny said.

"Uncle Feldman says mice have to expect things like that," Fendall replied. "Even with good luck, mice don't live to be very old."

"I didn't know," said Lonny.

"That's why he wants to have all the fun he can, while he can. Uncle Feldman is a great one for having fun."

"What does he do?"

"Anything, so long as it looks like fun. Of course, he's careful, too, or he wouldn't have lived as long as he has."

"I'd like to meet him," said Lonny.

"He avoids people as much as he can," Fendall said. "That's one of his rules for staying alive. In your case he might make an exception, but I don't know. Ah — is there by any chance another of those ginger cookies lying about? They're the best I ever tasted."

"I think so." Lonny went to the cupboard and reached into the cookie jar, but all he found were crumbs. "Sorry," he said. "I guess we're out."

"Ah, well." Fendall brushed his whiskers once more, washed his face, and curled up in the nest. "In that case, I'll catch a quick nap.

What with one thing and another, I didn't get much sleep last night."

"What time does your Uncle Feldman come by?" Lonny asked, but Fendall was already asleep. Lonny tiptoed from the room, and when he got outside he sat on the porch and wondered if he dared tell his parents. He wanted to tell someone, but he knew the boys in school would laugh at him, and he was afraid his parents would think he was making up a tall story. For some reason he couldn't understand, they were more afraid of his telling tall stories than almost anything else, and he decided not to risk it. He looked around the yard and his eyes lit on an old seesaw, which he and Bobby Bigelow, who lived nearby, had played on when they were younger. It was old and splintered now, but he remembered how much fun they'd had with it, and it gave him an idea. He went to the woodpile, found a thin piece of kindling about as long as his hand, then found another on which it could balance, and took them into the kitchen. He put them on the floor near the cage, and as he was balancing the one on top of the other Fendall awoke and looked at him.

"What's that?" Fendall asked.

"It's a seesaw," Lonny replied. "I thought your Uncle Feldman might like it."

"Can you eat it?"

"No, you balance on it. One of you gets at either end, and then you kind of bounce up and down. It's fun."

"It would be more fun if you could eat it," said Fendall. "Can't you smear something on it to make it taste good?"

"Try balancing first," Lonny replied. "If that gets dull, then we can try something else."

"It sounds too much like work," said Fendall, and he curled up and went back to sleep.

Next morning, however, Fendall was more enthusiastic. "Uncle Feldman thought it was great," he said. "He learned to balance all by himself."

Lonny looked around, and saw that the seesaw was gone. "Where is it?" he asked. "What did he do with it?"

"He took it back to his lair," Fendall replied. "He wants you to come and visit him tonight."

"How can I, if I don't know where it is?" Lonny asked.

"I'll take you. Just don't tell anyone."

At that moment, Lonny's mother came into the kitchen. "Did I hear you talking to someone?" she asked.

"You might have," Lonny replied.

"Who? I don't see anyone here."

"I was talking to the mouse."

Mrs. Stebbins gave her son a long, hard stare. "Are you all right?" she asked.

"Of course," said Lonny. "I told you, it's no trick to talk to a mouse. Anyone can do it."

Mrs. Stebbins continued to look at him, and then she glanced at the floor. Next she looked in the back room, in the onion bin, and then into the empty cookie jar. "Did you let him out of his cage?" she asked.

"Not me," Lonny replied. "I should say not."

"Then there's been another mouse around. I'm going to have your father put out more mouse seed."

"Don't do that," Lonny said quickly. "You might get Uncle Feldman."

"And who, if I may ask, is Uncle Feldman?"

"Another mouse," Lonny replied, as though

it were the obvious answer.

"Off to bed you go," his mother said, taking him by the arm. "I'm going to put an end to these wild stories, right here and now."

III

Well, I certainly outsmarted myself on that one, Lonny thought as he lay in bed. How am I going to meet Uncle Feldman if I don't know where his lair is and Fendall is penned up in a cage in the kitchen? I may have missed my only chance to see a mouse on a seesaw, because if they put out more mouse seed they may very well get Uncle Feldman the way they got the rest of the family, and that'll be the end of it. The thought made him sad, and he wondered how he could warn Uncle Feldman to stay away from the seed. If only I hadn't been so smart, he thought. Just because I can talk with a mouse, I thought I was smarter than anyone else. Maybe one of these days I'll learn.

Just as it was getting dark, and the birds were singing their good-night songs before settling in the trees, Lonny heard a sound on the window-sill next to his bed. He turned and saw Fendall's bright black eyes looking at him.

"Hey!" he said, sitting up. "How did you get out?"

"Not so loud," Fendall said in his small voice. "They think I'm still in the cage."

"But how'd you do it?"

"A mouse can squeeze through anything. You flatten your ribs."

"Did they put out more mouse seed?"

"Yes, but I told Uncle Feldman. He said not to worry; he never touches the stuff."

"Can I go see him?"

"Later. I'll come back when they're all asleep, and then we can go."

"Should I get dressed?"

"It might not be a bad idea. You can never tell what he may want to do."

The house was dark and quiet when Fendall returned. Lonny was lying beneath his covers

27

fully dressed, and although he thought he'd stayed awake he must have dozed off, because all at once he felt something soft on his cheek and heard Fendall say, "Anytime you're ready, we are." He sat up. Fendall clung to his shoulder and said, "Down in the cellar. And try not to make any noise."

With Fendall riding on his shoulder as a guide, Lonny tiptoed past his parents' room, where he could hear their deep and even breathing, and then down the staircase, through the front hall, and back toward the kitchen and the cellar door. It squeaked as he opened it, and Fendall tightened his grip. "Easy does it," he said. "You'll wake every cat in the neighborhood."

"Sorry," Lonny replied, and he crept quietly down the cellar stairs.

"Over by the furnace," Fendall said. "In back of the peat moss."

Lonny went to where his father had stored several bags of peat moss, and looked behind them. There, in the flickering light of the furnace, he could see Feldman Fieldmouse, balancing on the seesaw. He was standing upright, his forepaws behind his back, and maintaining his

balance by constantly shifting his tail. His head
was back in an attitude of sublime contentment,
and he opened his eyes as Lonny approached.

"I want to thank you for this gift," he said.
"Very few mice are as fortunate as I."

"I'm glad you like it," Lonny replied. Looking around the lair, he saw that Feldman had

brought some of the shredded paper from the rolltop desk, an apple and two onions, half a ginger cookie, a tangled mass of Mrs. Stebbins' knitting yarn, an old slipper in which to sleep, and a picture so small he couldn't identify it. "This is a nice place you have here," he said. "It looks very comfortable."

"It's makeshift, but it will serve," Feldman replied. "Of course, it's nothing like that old desk, but then — " He put one forepaw in front of his mouth, and coughed gently.

"I'm sorry about that," Lonny said. "I didn't want him to do it."

"Think nothing of it," Feldman replied. "It was too good to last. You know, we mice are a gentle breed; we can't understand why people hate us, but we accept the fact that they do, and make the best of it. One day I'll go back to the desk, when things have quieted down, and it will be like old times again — or almost. I like to say, the old times may have been good, but you should always look to the future. It's all right to remember pleasure, but it's even better to experience it." He closed his eyes again, and rocked the seesaw back and forth.

"That picture," Lonny said, indicating the small piece of paper. "What is it of?"

"It's not a very good print," Feldman replied apologetically. "I didn't do it, needless to say. I ran across it quite by accident."

"What is it of?" Lonny repeated.

"It's something I saw once, and it was so beautiful I'll never forget it. This human photographer clearly saw it, too, but I must say he didn't do it justice. You can barely make out what it is." Feldman paused, then went on:

"Once, at the full of the moon, I saw the rabbits do their moon dance. They form a circle and then, just for the sheer joy of it, they leap straight in the air and keep on leaping, still in a circle, until they're exhausted. I've only seen rabbits do it, and I've only seen it once, so I don't know if it's a habit with other animals or not. To the best of my knowledge mice have never been known to do it, and I think this is a crying shame. I've never seen such joy as was expressed by those rabbits, and that sort of thing ought to be shared by everyone. If the whole world could know joy like that, it would be a better place to live in."

"Uncle Feldman, may I have part of that ginger cookie?" Fendall put in. "I feel as though I haven't eaten in days."

Feldman looked at his nephew with mild distaste. "Here I'm describing something unutterably beautiful," he said, "and you're thinking about food. Have you no appreciation of the finer things?"

"Like what?" said Fendall.

"Like the moon dance!" his uncle exploded. "What did you think I was talking about?"

"I don't know," said Fendall. "I was thinking about the ginger cookie."

Feldman was quiet for a moment, and then he said, "I think maybe you've been too sheltered; if you ever have to fend for yourself, you'll be doomed. I think maybe you should look around a bit, and see how other animals live."

"Can't you bring them to me?" Fendall asked. "I can just sit in the nest, and they can tell me."

"Great leaping wharf rats!" Feldman shouted. "Is this what living with people has done to you? You're spoiled rotten!"

"You've always told me to enjoy things, and that's what I'm doing."

"Yes, but there's another side to every coin. You can't just loll about and expect people to wait on you."

"If they like to wait on me, why not?"

Feldman looked at Lonny. "This is partly your fault," he said, "but it's also partly mine. I didn't realize he'd take me so literally."

"I'm sorry," Lonny said. "I thought I was being a help."

"Well, I think a little trip to the pond may be good for us all," Feldman said. "Will you join us?"

"I'd love to," Lonny replied, wondering what would happen if his parents should awake and find him gone.

"Will there be something to eat at the pond?" Fendall asked.

"If you look for it," said his uncle. "And if you can get it before something else gets you."

"I don't like the sound of that," said Fendall.

33

"That, my boy, is because you've been spoiled. We'll take care of that."

"Is it wrong to be afraid of being eaten?" Fendall asked in a small voice.

"It's wrong to hide from facts. You stay where you are, and I'll come up on the young gentleman's head to guide him." So saying, Feldman sprang off the seesaw, zipped up Lonny's side, and perched on his head. "All right," he said. "To the pond. Go by way of the brook, and go very quietly."

When they got outside, the night was alive with sounds. Crickets chirruped and sang, tree frogs shrieked their shrill peeping noises, an occasional bullfrog sounded a deep "ga-blonk," and from somewhere in the trees came the call of a whippoorwill. Lonny was suddenly able to hear hoots and honks and whistles he'd never noticed before, and he was aware of the buzzing of millions of insects. It was like an orchestra, with each animal playing a different instrument and all of them combining to make one throbbing melody. With his eyes accustomed to the darkness, he could see things, too; he saw the zigzag flitter of a bat as it darted about catching insects, he could dimly see the path that led to the brook, and once or twice out of the corner of his eye he saw a rabbit that had stopped to watch him pass.

"I never knew so many animals came out at night," he said. "I thought they mostly went to sleep."

"Night is the time for the timid," Feldman replied. "Deer, rabbits, and mice all like to feed at night, because there's less chance of being seen. There are no hawks or people or dogs to worry about." He cleared his throat and added, "It is also the time of fang and claw. The predators are out at night. Foxes, owls, skunks —"

"Why do you worry about skunks?" Lonny cut in. "They won't do anything if you leave them alone."

"Ha!" said Feldman. "That shows how much you know. For people, a skunk is something that may make a bad smell. For mice, it's something that'll eat you if it gets a chance."

"Skunks eat mice?" said Lonny.

"Everybody eats mice," Feldman replied glumly. "You'd think there was no other food in the world. Mice are the main diet of all the

predators — even fish, like bigmouth bass, will eat a mouse if he's stupid enough to go swimming. That's why we have such big families, and so often — we have to keep ahead of the law of averages."

"I want to go home," said Fendall.

"Oh, be quiet," his uncle replied. "You'll go home when I say you can."

"I want to go home now."

"Then go. Do you think you can find the way?"

Fendall said nothing. Then from the woods came a high, warbling hoot, and Fendall let out a little squeak of terror and clutched Lonny's shoulder more tightly.

"Be quiet!" Feldman commanded. "That's just what he wanted you to do."

"Who?" stammered Fendall. "Who is it?"

"An owl. He makes that noise to frighten stupid mice, and then when they try to get away he hears them and swoops down and — as a matter of fact, I may be a little exposed here — " Feldman scurried down off Lonny's head and onto his other shoulder, just as a dark shape glided by overhead. "This is better," Feldman

37

continued, as the owl made one slow turn and went back to its tree. "He won't come close if I'm down here. Just stay still, Fendall, and nothing will happen to you." To Lonny, he said, "It's a new experience, going out with a person. You're protection I've never had before."

"I'm glad to do it," said Lonny. "It's new for me, too."

As they neared the brook they saw that the air was spangled with twinkling fireflies, and Feldman relaxed and leaned against Lonny's neck. "It's a pretty sight, isn't it?" he said. "It's too bad mice can't light up their tails like that. On second thought, perhaps it's just as well. But I do wish we could work something special, or exhilarating, into our lives. Like that moon dance of the rabbits — I'd like to know if any other animals do that. If they did, perhaps I might persuade a few mice to join me in organizing one."

"Is that a dance the fireflies are doing now?" Lonny asked.

Feldman coughed. "Not precisely," he said. "It's more a — well, you might call it a hunt."

As though to illustrate his point, a firefly came
and hovered near Lonny's shoulder, the under-
side of its tail glowing on and off in a slow puls-
ing rhythm. Feldman called to it. "Is there
something I can do for you?" he asked.

The firefly hovered closer, still blinking.
"You haven't seen Alice, have you?" it said.

"I'm not sure I'd know her if I saw her,"
Feldman replied.

"Or Eleanor?" The firefly sounded faintly
worried.

Feldman thought for a moment. "Again, I
couldn't say for sure," he said. "But I see there's
someone blinking at the same pace you are, right
down atop that bush. Might that be she?"

"It is!" the firefly cried. "It's Eleanor! I

thought she'd never get here!"

"My name is Doris," said the firefly on the bush, still blinking. "But I don't suppose that makes much difference."

"I knew a Doris once, in Trenton," the first one said, as it came in for a landing. "Perhaps she was a relative."

"Perhaps," said Doris.

"It is a small world, isn't it?"

"Agreed," said Doris.

"We're not needed here," Feldman said to Lonny. "Let's get on to the pond before the moon comes up."

"Is tonight a full moon?" Lonny asked, picking his way along the bank of the brook. It gurgled and trilled and tinkled like the music of a circus.

"No, the full moon's come and gone," Feldman replied with a far-off tone in his voice. "We'll have to wait a while before another."

"What happens at the pond?" said Lonny.

"You'll see," Feldman said. "Sometimes it looks like nothing, and sometimes a great deal. But there's always something going on."

As they approached the pond they heard the

hoarse grunt of a bullfrog, and then the splash of a jumping fish. The air was full of the peeping of the tiny frogs, and then suddenly there was a smack like a pistol shot; and everything went silent.

"What was that?" Lonny asked.

"A beaver," said Feldman. "He heard you coming, and slapped the water with his tail. It'll be a while before anything starts again, so you might as well sit down."

Lonny sat at the foot of a tree near the water, and waited. The crickets started first, then the peepers, and then the bullfrog grunted, and everything returned to normal. There was a crackling noise, and a gentle splash, and Feldman said, "Look there," and pointed to where a spreading line of ripples crossed the water.

"What is it?" Lonny asked.

"The beaver. He's carrying sticks to his dam."

"I'm hungry," said Fendall. "Is there anything to eat around this place?"

"Plenty," his uncle replied. "You'll find all sorts of tasties in the grass." Fendall started down off Lonny's shoulder, and Feldman continued,

41

"But don't get too close to the water, because that bullfrog sounds big enough to take you down in one gulp, and I can tell from here that the owl in that dead tree is watching us. You're better off staying where you are."

Fendall began to whimper. "Then how am I supposed to eat?" he said.

"Very carefully. You find a hole that you can hide in, and you burrow through the grass so nobody can see you. If you're seen, the odds are you'll be eaten." Then, as Fendall started to weep, his uncle added sharply, "And stop blubbering! It isn't all that bad. It just needs a little practice, and you'll find the food you work for tastes a great deal better than that you get for nothing."

"How am I going to practice if I'm eaten right away?"

"You wait, and you watch, and you learn. Now, be quiet. Here comes the beaver."

A round, furry head glided across the water trailing a V of ripples behind it, and the beaver clambered wetly onto the bank and headed for the underbrush muttering, "What a night, what a night! Some fine time I'm going to give those otters a piece of my mind. I'm going to tell them — "

"Excuse me," Feldman cut in, "did I hear you mention otters?"

"You did," the beaver replied, gnawing at the base of a bush. "And a good-for-nothing bunch of clowns they are, if you want my opinion." He shook the bush savagely, and continued to gnaw at it.

"What have they done?" Feldman asked.

"It's not what they've done, it's their attitude. You'd think there was nothing to do in the world but play, and get in the way of decent folk who're trying to do an honest night's work. Here I'm trying to repair the winter damage on my dam, and these clowns come dancing around, nudging and tickling and making stupid jokes." From far across the pond sounded a large splash, and then another, and the beaver said, "There they are now, going down their idiot slide. First frontward, then backward, then for all I know standing on their heads — you'd think going down a slide of wet mud was a sign of genius or something — " The bush broke free, and he lifted it over his head and started back for the water. "Well, all I can say is if that's genius they're welcome to it, and I ask nothing more than to be left alone. Live and Let Live is my motto, and if more people would—" He stopped as two shiny otter heads popped out of the water in front of him. "All right!" he snarled. "Get out of my way!"

"Well, if it isn't old Goosie!" said one of the otters. "Did you know you've got a tree in your mouth, Goosie?"

"Goosie Goosie Gander, whither do you wander?" said the other otter. "And if that isn't a rotten rhyme I never heard one."

"Out of my way," the beaver repeated. "I'm serious."

"You're not serious, you're stupid," said the first otter. "Anybody who eats trees gets splinters in his mouth, and his brains turn to cork."

"And leaves sprout out of his ears," said the other. "And squirrels nest in his nose — "

"Listen, you two, I've had enough," the beaver said. "Get out of my way, or you'll get this bush in the face."

"Goosie, that's a terrible threat," said the first otter. "Did you know you can be skinned and made into a top hat, just for uttering a threat like that?"

The beaver stamped into the water, and the two otters nudged him and jostled him for a moment, then let him go. As they watched him cross the pond, the second otter said, "Can you imagine living under a dam all winter with that one? He's got as much humor as a duckbilled platypus."

Feldman spoke up. "He doesn't think much of you, either," he said. "He thinks all you do is play."

The two otters regarded the mice and the boy for a moment, and then the first one said, "Is this a joke of some sort? Are you going to a costume party?"

"I'm showing these two around a bit," Feldman replied. "Their lives have been somewhat sheltered."

"If that beaver thinks all we do is play," said the second otter, "he should try sometime to catch a fish under the ice. That would change his tune."

"That's right," the first agreed. "All he eats is bark; he doesn't know what it's like to chase your food. See how he'd be trying to catch a water snake when there's nothing else to eat — or catch anything, for that matter. Then he'd realize you've got to relax every now and then, or you'll go crazy."

"I agree completely," Feldman said. "I'm all for having as much fun as you can, when you can. The older you get, the more you appreciate it."

"I didn't realize mice felt that way," said the first otter. "I thought you were a pretty dedicated group."

"We are, but — well, I'd like to bring a little beauty into our lives. Under certain conditions,

46

beauty can be positively exhilarating." Feldman paused, then said, "Have you ever seen the rabbits dance?"

The otters stared at him. "The what?" said the first.

"The dance the rabbits do at the full of the moon."

"The last rabbit I saw was chased into this pond by a fox," the otter replied. "He was doing no dance step I ever knew."

"I've seen it just once," Feldman said. "They gather in a circle, and leap as high into the air as they can. It's absolutely wonderful."

The otters considered this, then the second one said, "Personally, I'm not very big on leaping. Sliding and diving, yes, but the mere thought of a leap straight into the air gives me a backache."

"Well, it's more the idea, anyway," Feldman said. "The idea of a frolic at the full of the moon is something I just can't get out of my head."

"I hope you'll forgive my saying it," the first otter observed, "but for a mouse you seem to have some pretty big ideas."

"Even mice can have dreams," Feldman replied quietly.

"Of course," said the otter. "I didn't mean to sneer."

"Do otters do anything special at the full of the moon?"

The otters looked at each other for a moment, then the first one said, "Come to think of it, we did some pretty stupid things last week, or whenever it was. A whole mob of us gathered on the slide, and then someone had the idea we should pretend we were a freight train, so we started hooting and making clanging noises, and then — "

"Let's not go into details, should we?" said the second otter. "I blush every time I think of it."

"It's the moon that does it," Feldman said. "The full moon has an effect on everything that lives."

"It's nice to be able to blame it on something," the second otter said. "I thought we'd all blown our minds."

"Maybe that's what happens to the rabbits," the first otter remarked. "They're pretty stupid

48

anyway, and it probably doesn't take much to make them fly off the handle."

"They taught us something about the full moon in school," Lonny put in. "Its pull makes the tides high, and it also does things to people."

"I don't want a technical explanation," said Feldman. "It was a beautiful sight, and I wish mice would do it."

"Well, I see an unbeautiful sight, right behind you," said the first otter. "Duck, everybody — here's the fox!" He and the second otter sank beneath the water, and Lonny and Feldman and Fendall turned and peered into the bushes behind them. The moon, lopsided and tired looking, had begun to creep up through the trees, and in its faint light they could see two pale green eyes staring at them. The mice clutched Lonny's shoulders tightly, and Fendall was about to flee in panic when his uncle spoke. Feldman tried to sound casual, but a slight tremor in his voice betrayed his nervousness.

"Ah, there," he said to the fox. "Were you looking for something?"

For a moment the fox didn't answer. Then he said, "Yes. You."

"Well, here I am," Feldman replied, affecting a laugh. "What can I do for you?"

"Who's your friend?" asked the fox.

"Excuse me. This is my nephew, Fendall Fieldmouse. Fendall, this is Mr. — ah — Fox. Or is it Renard?"

"I mean who's the boy?" the fox said.

"His name is Lonny Stebbins," Feldman replied with more assurance. "And he happens to be my bodyguard."

The fox came forward a little, and sat down. The white fur on his chest made a light patch in the darkness. "Is he to be trusted?" he asked.

"Exactly as far as you are," said Feldman. "He will be as friendly as you are — no more and no less."

The fox thought about this. "That seems fair," he said. "What are you all doing here?"

"We came for a nighttime stroll. I'm showing the boys around."

"Is there anything you'd like me to show them?"

"Like what?"

"Whatever you want. I know my way around pretty well."

"Offhand, I can't think of anything."

"What about food? Is any of you hungry?"

"I am," said Fendall before his uncle could stop him. "I'm starving."

"Well, now," said the fox. "What would you like to eat? You name it, and I'll get it for you."

"Fendall, let me do the talking — " Feldman began, but Fendall was carried away.

"I'll eat anything you have," he said. "I'll eat cookies or seeds or bread or oatmeal or — "

"I tell you what," the fox put in. "You come with me, and you can take your choice. I've got a whole larder full. I've got — "

"Fendall!" his uncle shouted, as Fendall started to get down from Lonny's shoulder. "You stay where you are!"

"I am addressing myself to Fendall, not to you," the fox said coldly. "Please don't interrupt." To Fendall, he went on, "I have cakes and pies and cookies and dates. I have sun-dried raisins, and grapes from the vineyards of Alsace and of Italy. I have honey from Mount Parnassus, where the bees feed only on wild thyme, and I have — "

"Fendall!" Feldman shouted again, but Fendall didn't hear him. He was down on Lonny's knee, and about to jump into the grass.

"I have peaches and nectarines and mangoes and papayas," the fox intoned, crouching slightly. "I have bluefish and blowfish and blackfish and —"

"Grab him, Lonny!" Feldman shrieked, and Lonny reached down and caught Fendall in both hands just as he jumped for the grass. The fox sat up, scowling.

"What's the matter?" he said. "You trying to starve the kid, or something? You don't want him to have a little fun?"

"Your idea of fun is different from ours," Feldman replied.

"I'm glad I don't have an uncle like you," said the fox. "A regular old spoilsport. A party poop from the word go."

Feldman was unconcerned. "Keep hold of him, Lonny," he directed. "Don't let him go until our visitor has left."

"Oh, we're being hoity-toity, are we?" said the fox. " 'Our visitor,' indeed! Who was here first, if I may ask?"

"We were," said Feldman. "We've been here since before moonrise."

The fox glanced at the moon. "Big deal," he said. "I've been here since last July." Then he looked across the pond, and his voice softened. "Well, well, well," he said. "Look what I see." On the opposite shore, just stepping into a spot where the moonlight touched the water, was a doe, and behind her a gangly-legged fawn. The doe stood motionless, her large ears searching for the slightest noise, and when she was satisfied it was safe, she lowered her head and drank. The fox crouched, then vanished.

"I hope he tries it," Feldman said. "If he

so much as goes near that fawn, the doe will kick his brains out."

A chill made Lonny's back quiver, and he realized the seat of his trousers was damp from having sat so long in the grass. Then the chill reached his nose; it began to itch, and a sneeze exploded from him that almost blew Feldman off his shoulder. The doe leaped out of the water and, with the fawn staggering after her, disappeared crashing through the underbrush. There were other noises of retreating animals, and silence from the frogs and crickets.

"Well, that tears it," Feldman said, when he had regained his balance. "We might as well pack up and go home. It's probably time you were getting in, anyway."

"Can I get back on your shoulder?" asked Fendall from inside Lonny's cupped hands.

"If you think you've learned a lesson," Feldman replied. "Otherwise, you'll stay where you are."

"I've learned," said Fendall. "I just lost my head when he mentioned all that food."

"One thing we're going to work on is your sense of perspective," Feldman said. "You've got to see things in their proper light."

"It was that honey from Mount Parnassus that got me," said Fendall. "Where is Mount Parnassus, anyway?"

"It's a place for the gods," his uncle replied in his faraway voice. "Only a very few mice ever get there." He thought for a moment, then added, "Come to think of it, maybe that's where they do the dance."

IV

The next time they went out, Fendall was nervous before they'd even reached the brook. "Suppose the owl is there again," he said. "Or the fox. What'll we do then?"

"The same as we did before," replied Feldman. "So long as Lonny is with us, we have nothing to worry about." Fendall said nothing, and Feldman went on, "Sooner or later, you're going to have to fend for yourself, you know."

"What does that mean?" Fendall asked.

"That means you'll have to learn how to make out alone."

The idea startled Fendall, and his voice squeaked so high that Lonny could barely hear him. "How?" he asked.

"I'll have to work on that," his uncle replied. "Yours is a somewhat unusual case."

"I don't want to," said Fendall.

"Lots of people don't want to do lots of things," Feldman replied. "Nevertheless they do them, because they must."

"I have to go to the bathroom," said Fendall.

"No, you don't."

"Yes, I do."

"Then go."

"Where?"

"By the shades of the giant gopher!" Feldman exclaimed. "Do I have to do everything for you? Get down off Lonny's shoulder and go!"

"I want to go back to the house."

"You can't."

Fendall was quiet for a moment, "What's a gopher?" he asked.

"A burrowing animal. It lives on roots."

"Do owls eat it?"

"No. It lives under the ground."

"I wish I were a gopher."

"Well, you're not, so stop wasting your time. There are better things to wish for."

"Like what?"

"You might wish for a little courage. I'm ashamed to have Lonny hear you whining like this. Keep it up, and you'll give mice a bad name."

There was a brief silence, and then Fendall said, "I hear something. Something in the air."

"Of course you do," said Feldman. "The air is full of things."

"This is making little squeaks. Like a mouse caught by an owl."

"It is nothing like a mouse caught by an owl. Hear that once, and you'll never mistake it. What you hear now is a bat. In fact — " Feldman hesitated, and looked up at the star-studded sky. "There he is. See him?"

Fendall and Lonny looked, and saw a dark fluttering shape that zipped about in a wildly zigzagging flight. "What's he doing?" Fendall asked.

"Catching insects. The squeaks you hear are

his radar; he finds his way by their echoes." Raising his voice, Feldman called, "Ah, there, cousin! How's the hunting?"

The bat made a looping turn, then dove and circled above Lonny's head. "Who called?" it squealed in a slightly clogged voice.

"I did," Feldman replied. "Feldman Fieldmouse here. I just wondered how the hunting was."

"Rotten," said the bat. "Is it all right if I join you for a minute?"

"Please do," Feldman replied. "Be my guest." As the bat fluttered in and landed on Lonny's shoulder, Feldman went on, "This is my nephew, Fendall, and our — ah — traveling companion, Lonny Stebbins."

"Pleased, I'm sure," said the bat. It wiped one leathery wing across its forehead and said, "What a night! I don't think I've caught more than three hundred bugs since sunset."

"What's the problem?" Feldman asked. "The air seems full of them."

"They're there, all right, but I can't catch them. My bloody radar's on the blink."

"Oh?" said Feldman. "How did that happen?"

"I got a head cold, day before yesterday. Hanging upside down in a damp cave isn't the ideal way to sleep, no matter what anyone tells you."

"I certainly wouldn't like it," Feldman remarked. "I'm more for the creature comforts, myself."

"Well, I got this cold, and it went to my ears, and now they feel as though they're plugged up with cotton. Without my ears my radar's no good, so the only bugs I've caught are the ones I've literally bumped into. Believe me, it makes for a long night when you have to get your food that way."

"Have you tried vitamin C?" Feldman asked.

"I've heard that's good for colds."

"I'm not a fruit bat, or I would. Come to think of it, I might give it a try. If I could gag down some sort of fruit, it might help."

"The problem is to find it, this time of year." Feldman looked at Lonny. "Your father has a barrel of apples in the cellar," he said. "Do you think he'd mind if our friend here took a sample of one?"

Lonny thought for a moment. "To be honest with you, yes, he'd mind," he said. "But he wouldn't care if I took one. I can go back and —"

"Never mind your going," Feldman cut in. "What your father doesn't know won't hurt him. If he's going to lose an apple he's going to lose an apple, and we need you with us here." To the bat he said, "Go to the Stebbins place, right across the field there, and underneath the steps by the back door you'll find a spot where a shingle has split. You ease through there and go straight in until you reach the water pipes, then turn right and follow them to the boiler, which is in the cellar. Across the cellar, under the stairs is a barrel of apples. You can smell it a mile away."

60

"Well, well, well," the bat said. "You learn something new every day."

"I like to think so," said Feldman quietly. "By the way, do bats do anything special at the full of the moon?"

The bat sneezed. "There seem to be more bugs out then," he replied. "We eat better. Other than that, one night is pretty much like the next."

"You don't do anything special? Like a dance?"

The bat considered this. "Looking at it one way," he said, "we don't do anything BUT dance. All over the sky, every night. Why do you ask?"

"I just wondered. I'm conducting a survey."

"Well, speaking for myself, I'm a dancing fool; but I only do it to catch my food. And now I think I'll go look for those apples. Thanks for the tip."

They continued on toward the pond, and after a moment Feldman said, "There's a life for you. Hang upside down in a damp cave all day and then have to fly around all night snapping at bugs. I'd sooner be a fat-tailed shrew."

"What's that?" Fendall asked.

"It's the smallest known mammal. Two inches long, and ugly." He sighed, and went on, "When I was young, about a year ago, I used to wish — just like you, Fendall — that I'd been born something else. One day I'd wish I was a fox, the next day I'd wish I was a weasel, and one day I saw a horse and oh! how I wished I were a large, prancing horse. Then it came to me that if I'd been born something else, it might just as easily have been something I DIDN'T want to be — like our cousin the bat, there, or a star-nosed mole, or something really stupid, like a cat. I decided I was just as happy being a fieldmouse, because there's too much chance of making a change for the worse."

"Doesn't an owl lead a pretty good life?" Fendall asked.

"He has his problems, too. No, I'd rather bring fieldmousery to its highest possible point than go lurching off in some other area and possibly wind up a tapir, or a three-toed sloth."

"How do you bring fieldmousery to its highest possible point?"

"I think the moon dance would be a start. It's

something to aim for, anyway."

"Well, at least I can dream I'm an owl."

"Dream all you want. But don't try to hoot, unless you want everyone else to die laughing."

Fendall thought for a moment, then shuddered. "On second thought, I don't even want to dream I'm an owl," he said. "I'd like to pretend they don't exist."

"That's as good a way as I know to get yourself eaten," his uncle replied cheerfully. "Pretend they don't exist, and zango! you're off in mid-air with a broken back. I told you before: it's wrong to hide from facts."

"There's a lot one has to remember, isn't there?" said Fendall.

"Those are the first even semimature words I've heard you speak. Maybe you won't be a total loss, after all. Now, let's be quiet. We're coming to the pond."

Lonny tiptoed across the spongy grass, and sat at the base of the tree. The tree frogs and the bullfrogs and the crickets peeped and honked and trilled their chorus without interruption, and Lonny realized they were used to him now, and accepted his presence. He and Feldman and

Fendall watched the scene in silence. Suddenly there was a soft whoosh in the air, and Fendall screamed.

"The owl!" he cried. "He's got me!"

"What owl?" came a voice from the tree, and they looked around into the large, black eyes of a flying squirrel. It had come from the top of another tree, and was now clinging to the bark behind Lonny's head.

"I'm sorry for the noise," Feldman said. "My nephew isn't used to the night yet, and I'm afraid he's rather nervous."

"I've been called a lot of things in my time," said the squirrel, "but this is the first time I've ever been mistaken for an owl."

"Well, you fly like an owl," Fendall said defensively. "You made exactly the same noise."

"Begging your pardon, I don't fly." The squirrel reached out one forepaw and one hind paw, showing a long, furry flap of skin that stretched between them. "I glide. I climb to the top of a tree, jump off, then open up and glide wherever I want to go. I can steer with my tail." He flicked his long, feathery tail in illustration.

"That sounds like fun," said Fendall.

The squirrel shrugged. "Fun is where you find it. If I could really fly, like a bird, that would be one thing. Or if I didn't have all this loose skin I could swim, like an otter. I'm sort of halfway between, and it can be frustrating. It seems to me the otters are the ones who really have fun. But then — " He shrugged again.

"Speaking of fun," said Feldman, "I'm thinking of getting up a little dance among the mice come the next full moon. Would that sort of thing be of interest to you?"

"I don't know," said the squirrel. "How do you dance?"

Feldman cleared his throat. "Well, the way the rabbits do it is to leap in the air, just as high as they can and for as long as they can." He made little hops on Lonny's shoulder to illustrate. "They zoom into the air like sparks from a fire. They keep a circle of rabbits bounding and soaring and leaping, until finally they reach a kind of peak of ecstasy, and then fall back exhausted. To me, it seems like the essence of all life."

"I'll have to think it over," the squirrel replied. "You make it sound attractive, all right, but I couldn't do it quite the way you describe. I have to start from the top and go down."

"Maybe you could work out a variation of your own," said Feldman. "Do a loop or two as you glide."

"Maybe," said the squirrel, doubtfully. "It might take a little practice."

"And speaking of practice," Feldman said, looking at his nephew, "it's clear you're going to need some instruction before we come out again. If you can't tell an owl from a flying squirrel, you're a menace to the whole party."

"I'm sorry," Fendall said. "I really thought he was an owl."

"I'm sure you didn't do it on purpose, but

66

that doesn't change matters. You're simply going to have to learn."

"All right," said Fendall. "I'll try."

"I can't ask for more than that." There was a growl of thunder, and Feldman looked at the sky. Low, black clouds hung over the treetops, and a cool breeze had sprung up, bringing with it the smell of rain. "I think we'd best adjourn for the night," he said. "I am a mouse who likes his comfort, and that does not include long walks in the rain. Let's go."

V

Lonny slept late next morning, and when he got downstairs Fendall was not in his cage. He called, and he looked in the back room, and he went down into the cellar to Feldman's lair, but neither mouse was anywhere to be seen. Out of curiosity he went to the apple barrel, under the stairs, and saw one apple that had tiny fang marks all along one side. He took it out and put it in his pocket to get rid of later. He didn't dare ask his mother about Fendall, because if she knew a mouse was loose she'd tell his father, and then there'd be no knowing what might happen. So Lonny tried to look unconcerned and pretended everything was all right. But he was so worried that he didn't eat much, and his mother made him go to bed shortly after supper. He was looking out at the darkening sky, and thinking of all the nighttime animals that would now be waking up, when suddenly Fendall appeared on the windowsill. He looked tired, and not quite as plump as the day before.

"Where were you?" Lonny asked.

"What a day THIS has been," Fendall replied, leaning wearily against the sash. "Uncle Feldman's been teaching me to forage for food."

"In the daytime?" Lonny said, incredulous. "You mean out in the open?"

"No, no." Fendall settled down, and washed his face and whiskers. "He set up a practice course, out in the garage. He's had me tunneling through loose grass, digging shelter holes, identifying different kinds of seeds — the works. And all the time he played owl; he sat on a beam and pelted me with peach pits every time I showed myself. I've got a lump on my head the size of a robin's egg."

"Well, I suppose it's a good idea," Lonny said. "You couldn't do much for yourself before."

"I'll tell you one thing — food tastes better. And I don't mean food like cookies. I mean grain, and rice, and things like that. When you've crawled through a grass tunnel, dug your way through the earth, been bombed with peach pits at every turn — believe me, anything tastes good. Besides, there's a kind of sense of achievement. One of these days I'm going to run that course and not get hit with a single peach pit. And that, I can promise you, will be a day we will celebrate. We might even get some of that honey from Mount Parnassus, if we can find it."

"I'd like to watch you sometime," Lonny said.

"Do you mind waiting a while? I'd rather you didn't see me until I was a little better at it."

"Whatever you say."

"Uncle Feldman says if I come along fast enough, we'll have a go at the real thing when the moon is dark. I mean, with a real owl instead of peach pits, and all that sort of thing."

"Won't that be dangerous?"

"Yes."

"Aren't you afraid?"

Fendall paused. "I'm terrified," he said. "But I've got to do it sometime. He won't let me until he thinks I'm ready."

"Maybe if you wait a month or two, you'll be able to do it perfectly."

"There are two things against waiting that long. One is I don't think my nerves would take it; every time I get hit with a peach pit I think suppose that was a big, curved, owl's claw sinking into me, and I almost faint. The other thing is that even old and practiced mice get caught; so practice isn't everything. Practice just lessens the odds against you, to a point. After that, it's no use. You have to do the real thing."

"Still, it certainly can't hurt."

Fendall took a deep breath, and puffed out his whiskers as he let it out. "I don't know," he said. "I really don't know. I almost think I'd rather get it over with than wait around having nightmares about the owl. And it isn't only the owl, you know; it could be the fox, or a skunk, or a frog — it could be almost anything. I could get so busy thinking about the owl that I could walk straight into the pond and get eaten by a bass. When you have to think of all these things and eating your own weight in food every day, it can get to be quite a burden. I think I begin to see what Uncle Feldman means about the dance."

"How?"

"When your life is so full of unpleasant things, it's good to be able to relax for a while, and do something pleasant. When I was little — when you found me — I thought there was nothing in the world but eating and sleeping. That was all right as far as it went; but the world isn't made for people like that, and you have to accept a few worries here and there. That's one thing that makes the moon dance so important. And I want to be ready for it next full moon."

"You've certainly grown up in the last little while."

"Mice have to. It's grow up or get eaten — sometimes both."

"May I come with you when you make your real run?"

"Naturally. You're our protection. We feel much better when you're with us. And, to be frank, it will help steady my nerves to know you're there."

"All right, then. I'll wait until you're ready."

They went out on a night when there was no moon, and clouds covered the stars. Things seemed quieter than usual, and although a few fireflies winked here and there in the grass, the riotous feeling of their first trip was missing. It was as though everything — the animals, the trees, even the night itself — was waiting to see if Fendall would succeed, or be eaten. Fendall rode on Lonny's right shoulder, staring straight ahead and every now and then running his tongue across his lips, and on the other shoulder his Uncle Feldman tried to cover his nervousness by humming a squeaky tune.

From the dark trees by the pond came a soft who-hooo, who-hoooo, whoo, followed by a burst of maniacal laughter. There was a brief silence.

"Well, he's there," Feldman said, briskly. "He's practicing his different calls. That's good."

Fendall licked his lips, and said nothing.

As they approached the pond, Feldman directed Lonny to sit under the same tree as before. Then he crossed over to Lonny's right shoulder, and in a voice so small that only another mouse could hear it he said to Fendall, "When he sits down, wait for three minutes before you move. Then go down to his foot, wait again, and listen. There's a hole next to the big tree root that you can use for shelter. Go there, wait again, then start your tunnel. Head toward the lily pads in the pond, and when you feel the ground getting spongy, stop and come back. You'll find plenty to eat along the way. Remember: always try to keep grass over your back, and hold your tail close to your body. O.K.?" Fendall nodded, just as Lonny sat down and settled against the tree. "Three minutes from now," Feldman said. When the time had passed, he patted Fendall on the behind and gave him a tiny shove. "Off you go," he said. "Good luck."

Lonny found himself holding his breath in the silence that followed. He could feel Fendall moving slowly down his shirt, then his trouser leg, then to his foot, and then he could feel him no longer. He strained his ears for any sound, but there was none; and although he imagined he could hear Fendall moving through the grass he could also imagine a lot of other noises, none of them real. The silence was so complete that it rang in his ears.

A shriek tore the night apart, and then another and another, and Lonny's skin froze. He could feel Feldman pressing against his neck, and heard Feldman whisper, "That means he's hungry. Hold on."

There was no sound, but there was a sensation of movement in the air above them, and they could dimly see the outstretched wings of the owl as it circled the rim of the pond, weaving back and forth and listening for any movement below. It doubled back, hovered, then swooped over the area where Fendall was tunneling, doubled back again as though uncertain, then its wings rose and it plunged toward the ground. Feldman clutched Lonny's neck tightly, but the owl stopped its plunge short of the ground and rose again, its soft wings beating the air with a cottony sound. Feldman and Lonny let out the breaths they'd been holding, and the owl flew slowly to the tree, where it resumed its perch and clicked its beak in hunger.

"He ought to be at the end of his tunnel now," Feldman whispered to Lonny. "He should be heading back any minute."

As though it had heard him, the owl left its perch and dropped toward the lily pads, and Feldman could stand the suspense no longer. "You out there!" he called as loudly as he could. "Do you mind telling me what you're doing?"

The owl veered sharply toward the sound of Feldman's voice, and when it got closer it saw Lonny and stopped its glide, circled back, and lit in the grass.

"Who is that talking?" it asked.

"It is I," said Feldman, with precision. "Feldman Fieldmouse. I was wondering why all the aerial acrobatics."

"You ought to know," the owl replied. "If you'll just step out here, I'll show you."

"Thank you, no," said Feldman. "Does it make you feel proud?"

"What do you mean?"

"Does it make you feel big — are you proud

of yourself, picking on animals no bigger than your eye?"

"I eat what I can," the owl replied. "What I can, when I can, and where I can. Size means nothing to me."

"If you knew how silly you look, you might have second thoughts," said Feldman. "Diving and zooming, looping the looping, banking and turning — and all to catch a mouse that hardly makes a mouthful. Why don't you pick on someone your own size?"

"Don't think I haven't," said the owl sourly.

"I jumped a big blacksnake once, and it threw a few coils around me so I couldn't fly, and I was lucky to get away with my life."

"A pity you did," said Feldman. "My sympathies are with the snake. Not always, of course, but certainly on this occasion."

"What's with you, anyway?" The owl puffed out its feathers in anger. "For a field-mouse, you make awfully tough talk."

"And for an owl, you sound pretty stupid," Feldman replied. "I thought owls were supposed to be bright."

The owl seemed to be counting to ten. "If I knew who started that rumor, I'd give him a piece of my mind," it said, clicking its beak. "Just because our eyes look big we're supposed to be wise, so every time we do something that isn't very bright the whole world jeers. My brother once — " The owl stopped, and listened. "What was that?" it said.

"What was what?" Feldman replied. "I didn't hear anything."

"There's something moving in the grass." The owl cocked its head in different directions, listening.

"No, there isn't!" Feldman said loudly. "If there were I'd have heard it, and I haven't heard a thing! Tell me about your brother!"

The owl continued to listen for a few moments, then said, "What about my brother?"

"You were going to tell me something stupid your brother did, remember? You said the whole world jeers when you do something that isn't very bright."

"Oh, yes." The owl stopped, and listened again.

"Your brother!" Feldman prompted. "Tell us what your brother did!"

"Hmmmm? Oh, well, one time he jumped a porcupine." The owl chuckled. "Got a whole face full of quills."

"That's not so stupid," said Feldman. "Until you've brushed with a porcupine, I don't suppose there's any way to know. Those quills just look like wild hair."

"That's the first time," said the owl. "My brother did it twice."

"Well, he deserved to be jeered at," Feldman said. "I must say, that is stupidity above and beyond the call of duty."

"Yes, but because he's an owl it made it that much worse. The grackles booed him, the blue-jays went insane with laughter, the mockingbirds called him all sorts of names, the —"

"What sorts of names?" Feldman interrupted.

"Oh, Pincushion, Needlenose, things like that. And the crows have never let him forget it. Any time a crow sees him, it calls its friends and they all gather round and pester him. They're not fooling, either; they really rough him up."

"I wish I could find it in my heart to sympa-thize," Feldman said. "Unfortunately, I can't."

"I can tell you, being an owl is no bed of roses."

"Well, it does no good to feel sorry for your-self. If there's anything I hate, it's a blubbering owl."

"Try being an owl yourself sometime, and see how YOU feel."

"This is sickening," Feldman said. "Why don't you zoom off and catch yourself a cricket? That'll make you feel big again."

"Because I still think there's something in the grass here." The owl took a few steps, then stopped and listened. "And I think it's coming toward you. There's one way to find out." The owl spread its wings and rose gently — "and that's from the air — "

"Fendall, the hole!" Feldman screamed. "Run for the hole!"

Before the owl was properly airborne, Fendall streaked the last few feet and shot into the hole by the tree root. The owl wrenched itself around in the air and dived, but too late. It rose and circled, contemplating an attack on Feldman, but Feldman was nearly out of sight behind Lonny's right ear.

"You think you're smart, don't you?" the owl said.

"Not very," Feldman replied. "Just smart enough to fool you."

"Well, let me tell you something. Before you start congratulating yourself, come and take a look around the base of my tree. The ground is littered with the skulls of mice who thought they could fool me."

"Sorry, I have better things to do," Feldman said. But the owl had already left. It returned to its perch, and all that could be heard was the clicking of its beak.

Under Feldman's direction, Lonny put his hand over the hole in the ground, and Fendall climbed into it. Then Lonny brought him up and set him next to his uncle.

"How are you, lad?" Feldman asked; but Fendall was trembling so hard he couldn't speak. "You didn't do badly," Feldman went on in a soothing tone. "A little too much noise, perhaps, but that was just nervousness. Next time you won't be so nervous. You O.K. now?" Fendall nodded, still trembling, and Feldman gave him a pat. "Really, you did quite well," he said. "For many mice, their first trip out is their last. All right, Lonny, let's go home and celebrate."

As they crossed the field toward the Stebbins' house, Feldman looked up at the sullen black sky and said, "In about two weeks the moon will be full. Let's hope the weather clears by then, because if the rabbits can do a moon dance there's no reason the mice can't. And I think we should have something to mark Fendall's — ah — coming of age, so to speak."

"How are you going to convince the others?" Fendall asked. "You can't have a moon dance with just two mice."

"I'm going to point out that, with Lonny with us, there is no danger. The predators keep their distance, and we can do as we please. I can think of no greater thrill than to spring straight into the air, in the light of a full moon, and not care who sees me. It would be sheer ecstasy."

Fendall thought about this. "It might be a good idea to check with the rabbits," he said. "There may be a few things it would be useful for us to know."

Feldman looked at his nephew with admiration. "Now that," he said, "is what I call constructive thinking. Fendall, as of today it can at last be said that you have stopped being a man and have become a true mouse."

VI

During the next two weeks, Lonny didn't see much of either Feldman or Fendall. Feldman was campaigning for his dance among the other fieldmice, and Fendall was practicing his obstacle course in the garage to perfect his feeding technique (his uncle had later admitted that if he, Feldman, hadn't intervened with the owl, Fendall probably wouldn't have survived his first trip). Lonny moved Fendall's cage up into his bedroom to save any embarrassing questions from his parents about Fendall's comings and goings, and on the surface it seemed that everything was normal. The slight chill, which he experienced the first night, had turned into a cold that left a lingering cough; but it seemed that every spring he had a cough, and nobody thought very much about it. His mother fed him medicine and told him to bundle up when he went out, and his father said if he bundled up too much he'd just catch another cold. They said the same things every spring, and every spring he had a cough.

Then, the night before the full moon, Fendall appeared in Lonny's window. The almost-full moon was creeping up through the trees like a fat orange, and although the day had been pleasant, the night air was cool. Fendall looked trim and confident, and his voice no longer showed any trace of nervousness or indecision.

"It's all set," he said to Lonny. "Everything's go for tomorrow night."

"That's wonderful," Lonny replied. "What time do we start?"

"We want to go out tonight and look the place over. He'll make the final decision when he sees where the moonlight falls. Apparently, it's important to be in the full light of the moon."

"You mean you want me to come now?"

"If you don't mind. We feel a lot better when you're along."

Lonny began to get dressed, moving quietly so as not to wake his parents. He could tell that Fendall was excited, because Fendall's tail moved back and forth making a slow letter S in the air; and although Fendall tried not to show it, his excitement was catching.

"It's funny," Lonny said. "After all we've heard about the moon dance, to think we're finally going to see one."

"To do one," Fendall corrected him. "This one's for real."

"You're right," said Lonny, putting on his sneakers. "But will Uncle Feldman want me to dance, too?"

84

"He wants everyone to dance who feels like it," Fendall replied. "To him, this is the climax of his career — to be the mouse who brings a thing like this to others is a very heady sensation. I must say, I envy him."

"Do you think he'd like it if I danced?"

"I think he'd be enchanted."

Lonny felt a glow spread over him, and he smiled. "All right," he said. "I'm honored."

"You see?" said Fendall. "He's done something for you, too."

Lonny put on his belt, and reached for a sweater. "Your Uncle Feldman is a great man," he said, and then corrected himself. "Excuse me —mouse."

"There are those who think he's just a nut," said Fendall. "In fact, eighty percent of the mouse population of the meadow says he's dangerous. Some of them even tried to get up a committee to have him imprisoned, but luckily mice aren't very good at committee work. It's every mouse for himself, which in this case is just as well."

They went out, and were joined by Feldman behind the garage. He scampered up onto Lonny's shoulder, and as they crossed the field he looked at the moon. It had turned a cold white once it cleared the trees.

"It'll be about an hour later tomorrow night," Feldman said, squinting his eyes slightly. "Whatever time we figure is right tonight, we'll add an hour for tomorrow. We don't want to have to sit around and wait."

"How many are you going to be?" Lonny asked.

Feldman sighed. "The good Lord only knows. I must have approached fifty or sixty mice, and the first dozen or so were flat turn-downs. The idea just didn't appeal to them, and since they'd never seen the rabbits they couldn't imagine the glory of it. Some mice, I'm afraid, are woefully lacking in imagination. And, paren-thetically, my cousin Foster is the worst. Since Foster has never heard of a moon dance, it then follows that a moon dance cannot be any good, because only the things Foster knows are good, and everything else is therefore bad. I finally had to start dropping names — yours among them, Lonny — before I could get anyone even to listen to me. I've got perhaps two dozen firm

commitments, and another half-dozen or so who
are wavering. But believe me, it took work. If
it were for any lesser cause, I'd never have gone
through with it.''

When they reached the pond Lonny sat down
at the usual tree, and they waited in silence. As
the moonlight seeped through the trees and
brightened the grass and the water and the lily
pads, the night noises grew gradually louder.
The peepers peeped, and the bullfrog grunted,
but it was as though they were waiting for something, holding themselves in for a final effort.
Then the moon swung into view overhead, and

the chorus grew louder and louder, and the air rang with peeps and squeals and grunts and honks, and a patch of grass on the opposite side of the pond glowed as though hit by a spotlight. The grass was bright silver, and the bushes glistened with tiny spots that shone like a halo in the surrounding darkness. The whole area quivered as though it were suddenly alive, producing its own light.

"There it is!" Feldman said, pointing excitedly. "There's the place!" His eyes were bright, and he was so carried away that he hopped up and down on Lonny's shoulder, and almost lost his balance. "That's where we'll go! What time is it, Lonny?"

Lonny sneezed. "I don't know," he said. "I left my watch at home."

"Well, no matter. We can estimate by the time from moonrise. Did you ever see anything so wonderful? If it's like this tonight, just imagine what it'll be like tomorrow!"

They watched, with the chorus of night noises ringing in their ears, and after a few minutes the patch of grass began to grow dim, and shortly thereafter it was in shadow. Slowly the noises began to subside, and the doe appeared at the side of the pond, followed by her fawn. They drank quietly, and quietly departed.

On the way back to the Stebbins' house Fendall said, "By the way, Uncle Feldman, did you ever ask the rabbits about the dance?"

"I asked one," Feldman replied.

"And?"

Feldman paused. "He said he couldn't remember. He said he blacked out." After another pause Feldman added, "I think I see what he means."

VII

When Lonny awoke next morning, he took a deep breath and something stabbed his chest like a knife. He breathed again, and this time a rattling cough tore his throat, and he went into a coughing fit that left him weak and dizzy. His mother came into the room, put her hand on his forehead, and then hurried out. He could hear her go downstairs, and call Dr. Gatchell.

Dr. Gatchell came sometime during the morning; examined his chest, throat, ears, and nose; then tapped his back and told him to breathe deeply. The head of the doctor's stethoscope was cold, but it felt good because everything else about Lonny was hot, and the cold ring of metal had a soothing effect wherever it touched. Then Dr. Gatchell and his mother went out of the room, and he could hear them talking but couldn't hear what they said. He didn't really care, and drifted off to sleep.

Later in the day some medicine arrived, and he was given a dose of it and slept again, and when next he woke up it was getting dark. He looked at the sky, and suddenly with horror remembered the moon dance. He lay still for a moment, wondering what he was going to do, and it came to him that there was only one thing he could do — he had to get out of the house. He left the bed as quietly as he could and groped for his clothes, but they'd been taken away, and he had to open a dresser drawer to find clean ones. He was putting on his underwear when the door opened, and his mother came in.

"Lonny Stebbins!" she cried. "What do you think you're doing?"

"I have to go out," he replied, looking for his socks.

"You get back in bed this instant!" She took him by the arm, and he tried to shake her off.

"I have to go out!" he repeated. "Let me alone!"

"George!" Mrs. Stebbins called as she tried to wrestle Lonny onto the bed. "Come here! Quickly!"

"Let me alone!" Lonny shouted. "I have to go to the mouse dance!"

His father burst into the room saying, "What's the matter here, anyway?"

"I have to go to the mouse dance!" Lonny cried. "The mice are having a moon dance, and I have to be there!"

"Hold him, George," his mother said. "He's delirious. You hold him down, and I'll call the doctor."

His father fell across him on the bed, and held his arms tight while he made soothing noises, and the more Lonny struggled the tighter his father held him. His father looked frightened, and the fright must have given him extra strength, because in the end Lonny could move only his head, and that not very much. His father kept repeating, "All right, all right, all right," as though he were talking to a baby.

There were lots of voices, and slamming of doors, and then someone scrubbed his arm with something cold and he felt the prick of a needle, and nothing more.

When he awoke next morning, his mother was at the foot of his bed.

"How do you feel?" she asked.

"All right," he replied. His chest felt tight, but he was no longer dizzy, and he seemed to have come back from somewhere very far away. His mother put a thermometer in his mouth, and he looked at the ceiling and breathed through his nose while she consulted her watch. Then she took the thermometer out, looked at it, and shook it down. "Do you feel like any breakfast?" she asked.

"I guess so," said Lonny. She left the room, and after a moment he turned his head and looked at the window, and there was Fendall on the sill. Fendall seemed old, and quiet, and for a while neither of them spoke.

"What happened?" Lonny asked.

"Well, we had the dance," Fendall replied. He closed his eyes.

"What happened?"

"I tried to tell him not to do it, but he wouldn't listen. I told him you must be sick because I couldn't wake you, and he said it didn't matter. The moon had got to him, and I guess he must have blacked out, like the rabbits. He insisted we do the dance." Fendall paused, then he added, "And I must say, for a while it was great. The light was even brighter than the night before, and the mice bounced up and down in it like furry fireflies. Once they got started they bounced higher and higher, each one reaching up into the night as though headed for the stars, and there didn't seem to be any coming down — all I remember was going up, then going up again, then going up still higher. I don't remember ever coming down."

"Then what?"

"The owls came, and the foxes. I don't know how many there were, but they seemed to come at us from all sides, as well as from above. I've never seen so many owls — or foxes either, for that matter. Everywhere I looked — " his voice trailed off.

"How many escaped?"

"A few. I got under a lily pad, and stayed there until it was over. I don't know about the rest."

"Uncle Feldman?"

"He was still dancing when the owl got him. The others tried to get away, but Uncle Feldman kept on leaping, going higher each time, and the owl picked him off in mid-air and took him to the tree. I tried not to listen."

There was a silence; then Lonny said, "What are you going to do now?"

"The same as any other fieldmouse, I guess."

"You're welcome to stay here."

Fendall shook his head. "Thanks, anyway. I've outgrown that kind of living." He hesitated, then said, "As a matter of fact, one of these days I might try to organize a dance, kind of in honor of Uncle Feldman. You can say what you like, it was a tremendous experience. I never knew there could be anything like it. And maybe this time —"

"Maybe I'll be there to help."

"Maybe. I don't know. But I think Uncle Feldman would like it if he knew someone had seen the same kind of beauty he had, and was willing to risk something for it. It's the risk that makes it worth doing."

"I guess you're right."

"Well — " Fendall wiped his whiskers, then rubbed his front paws together. "Take care of yourself, now." He seemed embarrassed.

"I will," said Lonny. "You, too."

"And thanks for everything. If there were more people like you, we mice wouldn't have such a gritty time." There were the sounds of Lonny's mother coming upstairs with his breakfast. Fendall waved once, then slipped over the windowsill and out of sight.